Dedicated to my nieces and nephew:

Rachel, Holly, Libby and Addison.

I love you all so much! x

And huge thanks to Lilly!

Scholastic Children's Books
An imprint of Scholastic Ltd
Euston House, 24 Eversholt Street, London, NW1 1DB, UK
Registered office: Westfield Road, Southam, Warwickshire, CV47 0RA
SCHOLASTIC and associated logos are trademarks and/or
registered trademarks of Scholastic Inc.

First published in the UK by Scholastic Ltd, 2017

Text copyright © AmyLee33, 2017
Illustrations by Luke Newell © Scholastic Children's Books, 2017

The right of AmyLee33 to be identified as the author of this work has been asserted by her.

ISBN 978 1407 17224 8

A CIP catalogue record for this book
is available from the British Library.

13 5 7 9 10 8 6 4 2

This is a work of fiction. Names, characters, places, incidents
and dialogues are products of the author's imagination or are used
fictitiously. Any resemblance to actual people, living or dead,
events or locales is entirely coincidental.

www.scholastic.co.uk

CHAPTER 1

The crashing waves beneath me do nothing for my growing fear. I can feel them hitting the old ship with a sound like thunder.

As I inch backwards along the plank, a sharp blade pointing at my chest, I scan the sea below.

Dark, formidable shadows swim close to the surface.

No way, I think, *it can't be!*

As their fins break the surface, the giant sharks circle below, waiting for their meal.

I shudder.

"Time's up, Princess," snarls Captain Silverbeard. "Tell me where you hid the enchanted jewels, or you are shark bait!"

I gulp. I can never reveal the location of the jewels.

The blade of the cutlass pokes my tummy as my heels hang over the plank.

"Never!" I shout, with every bit of strength I can muster.

"Very well," he spits. "But before you die, I want your last thought to be this." He pauses as he removes his eyepatch to reveal an empty socket. "Amy..." he says, "I am your father."

The words hit me like a bucket of ice-cold water running down my back. I know them to be true.

"Noooooooooo!" I scream.

I fall backwards into the water, the old captain watching me from the plank. As I turn midair, the sharks snap their jaws. I

flap my arms and legs, desperately trying to slow down. A great white lunges out of the sea, splashing me with cold seawater. I try to grab the air, I try to fly, but it's no use. The great white opens his jaws as I fall.

★★★

I wake up, drenched in a cold sweat, my heart beating fast, out of breath.

It was a dream. Just another dream.

The moon fills my bedroom with silver light. I sit up and rub the sleep from my eyes and scan my bed. Nine sleeping dogs act as my comforter. Lola, Romeo and Destiny keep my toes warm. Max and Mars stay on either side of me, no doubt wanting to stay close to keep me safe. Sailor is laid out on his back, his chest moving up and down with shallow breathing while Lexi is cuddled up to Luna. Boomer is sleeping on his back, his head hanging over the edge of the bed with his tongue out. I smile at my sleeping pups.

I climb out of the bed − ninja-style, careful not to wake them − and step outside to the balcony. A full moon hovers above the far-off Alpine Mountains. The air is cool, and I wrap my arms around myself. I notice a tiny pool of golden light just beyond my feet. My tiara is glowing again. I take it off and run my fingers over the bright jewel.

The dreams are getting more frequent.

Dreams about family. Where I come from.

No, Captain Silverbeard is not my father. But the dream's message is loud and clear: I must know where I come from. I must fill in the blacked-out memories of my past. I'm ready to know.

With a final look at the moon, I turn back to my bedroom and take care to avoid stepping on the tails of my cats – Saturn, Comet and Star – as I crawl back into bed.

Mars stirs, his sleepy eyes finding mine.

"It's OK," I whisper. "Go back to sleep."

He gently licks my cheek before his eyes close and he goes off into his own little dream world. And I guess I should go back into mine.

CHAPTER 2

The sun warms my eyelids in the morning. I lift my blankets over my head as I attempt to fall back asleep, but – hearing a thud and a yelp on the floor – I realize I must have somehow pushed off one of the dogs. I sigh as the fallen dog now barks with the excitement of being awake to start a brand-new day.

"Five," I mumble.

"Four." I hear sleepy whines of

many dogs awakening from their slumber.

"Three." The paws start moving above me.

"Two." A tail or two smacks me in the face.

"One." I get crushed by nine very awake and excitable dogs.

"OK, OK, I'm awake," I sigh, as I pull the blanket from my face. I sit up and rub my eyes as the dogs wriggle around like fish out of water. How do they have so much energy first thing in the morning?

The sun pours into my bedroom in beams of bright light. The cats don't stir – oh, how I wish I could sleep like them! If it isn't nightmares about Captain Silverbeard or the Witch, it's my dogs waking me up!

I step outside on the balcony once more and feel the morning sun on my face. I smile gratefully as I look down at my Land of Love, like I do every morning. The Cute Recruit patch, the farm, the jungle, the large mountai—

WAIT A MINUTE.

My brain suddenly wakes up as I spot something out of place at the Cute Recruit patch. There is something there… I squint my eyes, trying to make sense of whatever it is. Something blue … and moving! It's a person! Or at least it looks like a person. A person with a blue pointy hat.

The Witch?

No, not the Witch.

Suddenly, the figure disappears with a popping sound.

Confused, I rub my eyes. But whatever was there is not there now.

Hmm. I wonder if maybe I was just imagining things again. Sometimes I get a little too carried away with my daydreams.

Yeah, maybe it was just that.

After feeding the dogs and cats their breakfast, it's time to pick my sidekick for the day. The dogs all line up like little

soldiers, looking their best and giving their most innocent

faces to show that they won't be any trouble.

"Today I'm going to pick … Max!" Max

jumps into my arms and gratefully

licks my chin. "And I want to

take Saturn with me too!" My

first cat, Saturn, purrs as he

leaps over the heads of the dogs

and headbutts my knee.

The remaining dogs begin to

whine, sad that they were not chosen.

"Don't worry, guys, we will be back in a few hours, OK?"

I pat each of their heads in turn before leaving with Max and

Saturn.

After giving my huge, soldierly iron golems, Bert and Bertha, a morning cuddle, I make my way to the snow golems' room. I peer through the window in the door to see if I can make out any traps or pranks Mittens may have prepared to greet me, like a snowball in the face or, his recent favourite, dropping a pumpkin head on my head. The last time it was so stuck Bert had to pull it off for me!

I see Mittens, Mr Frost and Blizzard standing with their backs to me, staring out of the window. Now, this could be a decoy. Mittens has made fake snow golems before by putting together two big snowballs and a pumpkin head, to distract me while he comes out of a hiding place and slams a pumpkin on my own head. Mr Frost and Blizzard are not so innocent themselves; I don't see them stopping him!

I gently push open the wooden door, my eyes scanning the room for any mischief. But there appears to be none … for now.

"Good morning, you lovely, lovely golems!" I greet them.

Mittens, Mr Frost and Blizzard turn to me and smile with their toothy pumpkin mouths before turning back and staring out the window once more. Curious, I stand next to Mittens.

"It's him!" I scream. I press my nose against the window, staring in disbelief. Standing on the wall of the farm is that blue figure from earlier!

"You see him too, right?" I ask the golems, who all nod. "I knew it! I knew I wasn't crazy!"

He appears to be a man wearing a blue dress. No, not a dress, a cloak. And a pointy blue hat. Almost like the Witch's hat. "Who is he?" I whisper. And then, just like before, he suddenly vanishes into thin air.

"Darn it!" I need to know what's going on. Maybe he will come back if I go out there?

"Have a good day, you guys!" I say, turning to leave the room. "See you later!" Just as I open the door to let myself out, a freezing-cold snowball hits the back of my head and slips down my neck, sending icy chills all down my spine!

"MITTENS!!!" I screech.

★★★

Grabbing my backpack and my trusty bow, Katniss, I head outside with Saturn and Max following.

Grandfather Oak, my dearest friend, stands tall in the morning sun.

"Good morning, Grandfather!" I say as I reach my favourite tree.

A wide smile across his trunk, Grandfather Oak beams down at me. Each crack in his bark moves with his smile. "Good morning, Amy dear. How are you?"

I quickly look behind him, my head snapping from left to right, scanning the river and beyond. "Erm… I'm good," I say.

"You seem rather distracted today," Grandfather Oak notices.

Something catches my eye, and I spin around – only to find Max and Saturn playing leapfrog behind me.

"Oh yeah… I keep seeing someone here, in the Land of Love. I don't like it."

"Really? How wonderful! A new friend, perhaps?" Grandfather Oak says.

"I don't know; I don't trust him."

"Well, what do we know about him?" he asks.

I think for a moment or two.

"Nothing, I guess."

"Well, maybe we should greet our visitor with a smile and offer him some tea?"

Grandfather Oak, always so kind and trusting. I guess I

shouldn't jump to conclusions and assume the visitor is here to turn me into fairy dust. Maybe he is a good egg.

"Let me tell you a story," my friend says.

Feeling excited at the thought of a new story, I smile and sit cross-legged on the grass, with Max snuggling on my lap. Saturn leaps up and perches on Grandfather Oak's longest branch, looking rather like a black panther in the jungle.

"This story may help you understand why we should always assume people have good intentions," he says.

I feel my cheeks grow slightly pink. Usually, I don't need reminding of such values, but ever since the Witch cast the Darkness Hex on my land, I have become much more … *cautious.*

"This story begins with a rabbit called Cleo, a fox called Rex and a raccoon called Luka."

I forget my troubles and immediately imagine what the

rabbit, fox and raccoon look like. Stories about animals are my favourites!

"Each night, the three young animal friends gather around an old tree for a night-time story. The animals are very protective of this tree, Old Red, and when one night a strange badger emerges from behind Old Red, the animals immediately feel defensive. The old badger—"

"**ITS HIM AGAIN!**" I jump up and grab Katniss. Max picks himself up, having abruptly fallen off my lap.

Standing on the other side of the bridge, across the squid lake, is the stranger.

"He's not getting away this time!" I say, narrowing my eyes and running towards the bridge. Saturn leaps from Grandfather Oak's branches on to my shoulders, his claws clutching my clothes.

"Remember to be kind, Amy," I hear Grandfather Oak say.

I know, I know.

I know to always be kind. I am kind. But I can't help be nervous, suspicious. It's like the Witch had planted something in me when she released the dreaded Hex.

As I reach the wooden bridge, the blue-cloaked man is still on the other side, with his back to me. Max leaps in front, snarling, as I load an arrow on to Katniss. The bridge sways slightly, and the creaking wood brings me back to my nightmare on the ship with Captain Silverbeard.

I slowly make my way closer to the man, as giant squids swim below me. Saturn's claws grip tighter to my clothes, and I can feel them prick my skin.

As I get closer, Katniss's arrow pointing ahead, I can hear him making a muttering noise. Is he talking to himself? His blue cloak is shiny; it catches the sun, making him look electric.

Now just yards away, I stop. Confused.

"Ah, yes, well. Indeed. Very late," he mumbles, and I hear the pages of a book being turned frantically.

His voice… I recognize him! I lower my bow as I try to think back to where I have seen him before.

Max, who is still wary, barks.

"Arrrghh!" The man turns and screams in fright, then cowers beneath his long sleeves, dropping his book.

"Hey, it's OK, he won't bite," I say. Max looks at me and understands. He stops snarling but remains on guard.

The man quivers as his giant nose and huge glasses peek over his shaking arm. "I'm sorry, barkhounds make me nervous!" he says, his voice wobbly.

Barkhounds? What on earth is that? I wonder.

Suddenly, he stops quivering as his eyes grow large. His grey moustache twitches as his pupils expand. "Princess Amy!" he whispers.

Suddenly, he flings himself at me and I am swallowed by the many layers of his cloak.

"Oh, Princess, it has taken me so long to find you again! You woke up late! You should have been at the Cute Recruit patch forty-five minutes ago!"

I try to respond but can

barely breathe with his cloak choking me. Saturn seems to be wrestling the waves of the cloak, and I hear Max growl. As the man pulls away, with Max gripping the bottom of his cloak in his mouth, I cough and rub my throat. Saturn jumps down and begins to groom himself, displeased that his fur has been disturbed.

"Oh!" I say as a memory hits me. "You're the Wizard guy who took me through the portal to show me my destiny when I became a princess."

The Wizard stands proudly as he pushes his glasses back up his nose. "Indeed, I am!" He beams.

A long time ago, this Wizard guy appeared and informed me that I must travel through a portal where I would meet my destiny. I was scared, but I did it – and found out I come from a long line of princesses! I haven't seen him since.

"What brings you here again?" I ask.

Suddenly, his face changes. His pink cheeks turn white and his moustache droops like a cat's whiskers.

"Well … er … Princess, you are in very grave danger."

My mouth falls open.

"What? AGAIN? Aw, dude, come on!"

CHAPTER 3

"Er, yes, I'm afraid so. And we don't have much time!" The old Wizard shakes his head and stoops to pick up his fallen book.

I sigh. "What is it this time? Werewolves? Oooooh, I bet it's werewolves! I wonder if I could tame one... I could call him Fluffy, and he would be my new best friend, and then—"

"Amy, it's not werewolves."

My daydream of a new puppy is cut short.

"Cowboy aliens? Grandfather Oak once told me a night-time story about cowboy aliens. This one time, they went to Jupiter and—"

"It's about the end of the world."

I shake the cowboy aliens from my mind as the old Wizard's milky blue eyes fill with sadness. Or fear. Or maybe both.

"The end of the world?" I ask, my voice wavering.

"Let's not talk here. May we go somewhere to sit down? I am so very tired."

I suddenly remember Grandfather Oak's advice earlier, and notice just how exhausted the old Wizard looks. I gently put my arm around him and guide him towards the Gingerbread Teahouse for some tea.

Although I feel anxious, I don't feel fear … yet. Ever since the Darkness Hex, I have felt a change in myself. No longer afraid of my own shadow, I feel stronger. Braver. Confident.

Like I have grown up all of a sudden. I'm not a little girl any more.

I feel the weight of the Wizard on my shoulder as we walk past the river of chocolate, the giant mill churning away. Max has the bottom of the Wizard's cloak in his mouth, trying his hardest to help. I smile at my sweet dog. Saturn, meanwhile, strolls on ahead, his tail reaching to the skies above, turning his nose up at the autumn leaves crunching beneath his paws.

"Here we are!" I say as I push open the door to the entrance. The smell of candy fills my nose as I guide the Wizard to a chair by the roaring fireplace.

"Thank you, Princess," he says as he sighs with relief. "I forget I'm not a hundred and eighteen years old any more!"

"Wait ... what?" Did I hear that right? "How old are you?" I ask.

The old Wizard chuckles. "My dear princess, in a world full of magic, full of witches and golems, zombies and talking trees,

does my age really come as a shock?"

He sure has got me there! "I guess not! So are you, like, five hundred?" I ask.

"Come on, now, don't be cheeky, Princess! I may be old, but I'm not *that* old!" He chortles. "No, dear, I am one hundred and forty-five years young."

A sudden thought occurs to me as I fill a teapot with water: "So, wait a minute, you must have been around before! Before I came to the Land of Love. You must have seen when the Witch ruled it before me, when the shadows reigned."

The old Wizard nods as he strokes Saturn's head, who has now perched himself upon the Wizard's knee.

"So then you must know how I came here! You must know my family!" I can feel excitement rise from my toes to the top of my head at the very thought of finally getting some answers.

"Alas, no, my dear," he answers. "I travel through many dimensions, many portals, many worlds. When the Witch reigned over this world, a prophecy was already in place to protect it, and to protect you, when you would arrive. I was needed elsewhere, my dear."

The excitement drains from my head and back out through my toes. As the teapot screeches on the oven, I put together a tray of teacups, milk, sugarcubes and freshly baked chocolate cupcakes and join the Wizard by the fireplace.

The Gingerbread Teahouse is by far my favourite place to visit in my land. A warm, cosy and inviting building crammed full of cakes, sweets and chocolate! On a cold, rainy day, I just love to come here and sit in the big armchair by the roaring fire and write stories, with a hot cup of peppermint tea and a big slice of carrot cake.

I pour some tea into each of our cups, and pass one to the Wizard, who takes it gratefully.

"OK, so what's with the new end-of-the-world thingy?" I ask, as I stir in some sugar.

The Wizard takes a deep breath, holding on to his teacup firmly. "There are many dimensions other than this one. Thousands, in fact. Different worlds, if you will. There are some creatures, wizards included, who have the ability to travel through most of them. We are not gifted in the magical arts for fun, my dear. We each have a job, to keep the worlds at peace. I am a guardian." The Wizard looks rather smug as he sips his tea.

Then he continues, "As you are well aware, there is light and dark, day and night, good and bad. And this is in every world, not just yours. It is my duty as a guardian to stop creatures from entering a world where they do not belong, or to safely guide visitors, as I did with you many years ago."

I nod, trying to keep up while nibbling on a chocolate cupcake.

"We call those creatures who try to sneak in 'Hitchhikers'.

It is my job to stop these Hitchhikers from causing chaos. who knows what disasters could occur if a creature such as a wrifflon entered here!" He chuckles.

I sit up straight. "I'm confused. What on earth is a wrifflon?" I say, my mouth full of cupcake.

"Exactly. They are not of this earth! The very imbalance could disrupt everything. It would be the same if you travelled to 842.zPK." The old Wizard takes another sip of his tea.

"What the heck is that?" I ask, my voice somewhat higher than usual.

"Ah yes. 842.zPK is a wonderful world!" The old Wizard smiles as his eyes glaze over with reminiscing. "One of my favourites, in fact! I love to just see the fillynewts in their natural habitat, flying around in the sea…"

I drop my cupcake. "Flying around in the—"

"What I mean is, if you travelled to 842.zPK, you might perish. Or you might shrink to the size of an ant. You might not be able to breathe the same air; the water might be poisonous to you. Your very presence may disrupt everything. Which is why guardians stop Hitchhikers from entering different worlds." The Wizard pauses to stroke Saturn, who looks very annoyed that the Wizard had stopped stroking before, in order to drink his tea.

"Are you familiar with the butterfly effect?" the Wizard asks.

"Erm, no," I answer.

"Well, the butterfly effect refers to how one small change, such as the flutter of a butterfly's wings, can result in large differences. Adding just the smallest bit of wind from the wings of a butterfly could make the weather grow, eventually, into a hurricane. So we guardians do our best to protect worlds even from small changes that could grow to become catastrophic. And our ancient laws dictate that we do not intervene in the worlds we protect, for the same reason."

I rub my forehead and blink several times, trying to take

this all in. Surely, I am dreaming. I add another spoonful of sugar to my tea.

"As I said before, there is good and bad in every dimension," the Wizard continues. "Each dimension has its own world, its own history, its own way of doing things. And yours, my dear, has changed dramatically of late. Since the Darkness Hex, your world oozes power. It has become a hot spot, if you will, for those who seek magic. You have no idea how many gullypaxes, hornkogs and fillynewts I have had to keep out of here."

"What are … never mind." My head falls to the table with a thud in confusion.

"But there has been a new evil rising." The Wizard looks down sadly. "An evil that jumps from world to world, taking their powers and bleeding them dry. The guardians have failed to stop it, and it's heading this way."

"I don't understand. What do you mean by power?" I ask.

"The power the Witch and you yourself created in the battle of good and bad. Love and hate are the most powerful forces, and your world took in this power. Its magic runs through the rivers, grows in every blade of grass, is present in every tree."

I say nothing for a few minutes. Slowly digesting what the Wizard is telling me – slowly, hypnotically stirring my now-cold tea as Max eats my fallen cupcake.

"What is this new evil? Is it a creature?" I ask.

The Wizard takes a deep breath, and pulls a heavy, leather-bound book from inside of his cloak. He turns a few pages before laying the book down and pushing it towards me. There, printed in the old book, is what I can only describe as a monster. Sketched in black ink, the monster stares up at me

from the old yellowed page. A large, black round body, covered in scales, with two huge pointed horns on the top of its head towering over two smaller horns in front. Giants claws on each hand, a thick tail with a pointed arrow tip. But its face … its face is haunting. Its eyes are white, and its mouth is spread in a huge white grin, like a jack-o'-lantern.

"It's a Megalo. Megalos desire power. And they stop at nothing until they get it, destroying whole worlds," the Wizard says.

"Megalo," I whisper.

"And the most powerful Megalo of all is on its way."

I gulp.

We sit in silence. The only sound I hear is the wood crackling in the fire. A now sleepy Max, full of cupcake, is curled around Saturn, both basking in the warmth of the fire. I smile to myself as every time Max breathes out on to Saturn's ears, they twitch.

"What will the Megalo do?" I ask. I can feel my eyebrows furrow.

The Wizard takes off his glasses and cleans them with the sleeves of his cloak. "The elder guardians have been researching Megalos for many centuries. They are very rare creatures, and we know very little about them."

I glance at the drawing of the Megalo. Its terrifying smile

makes my tummy fill with butterflies. *A different butterfly effect,* I think to myself.

"What we do know is this: the more power Megalos take, the bigger and stronger they become. I know a guardian who came across a small Megalo trying to get into another world. It was no bigger than Saturn here." The Wizard pointed to my purring cat. "It was an infant with no power, so it was relatively easy to stop. Simple defence magic fought it off, so we know magic – especially dark magic, which we do not possess – is an effective weapon against them."

I imagine a teeny tiny monster – and instantly feel guilty for thinking it would be cute!

"Our problem is, the Megalo heading to the Land of Love

is the largest one ever documented. And so far, the guardians have failed in protecting the dimensions that this Megalo has attacked." The Wizard looks down, sorrow written across his face. "We have lost many guardians, Princess. And many worlds destroyed. Obliviated. Gone. For ever."

I stare at the Wizard in shock. I forget to breathe as his words wash over me.

The Wizard sniffs and wipes his eyes with the back of his hand before putting his glasses back on. "I'm afraid that even the combined magic of the guardians is not enough to stop this creature. It will take more magic – and a lot of dark magic – to stop this Megalo. And there is only one being in this land who is wicked enough to stand a chance."

"Wait, are you saying what I think you're saying?" I ask, as the realization starts to hit me.

"Yes, Princess. We need the Witch to save the Land of Love."

CHAPTER 4

"Are you crazy?" I say in shock, standing up. The teacups wobble as I slam my hands on the table. I look at the Wizard in disbelief.

"I'm afraid not, Princess. I believe combining the very two forces that have enriched this land, good and bad magic, will be your only chance if – when – he gets through. The Witch needs to teach you everything she knows, to prepare you for the fight."

My mouth falls open. He wants the Witch to teach me

her magic. HE WANTS HER TO TEACH ME?! I begin to wonder about his sanity.

"You have got to be joking! You want the Witch and me to … what, team up? You do realize she only recently tried to destroy the Land of Love!"

"Yes, I know, Princess, I witnessed it all," he says. "You were very brave."

"You witnessed it?!" I shout angrily. Max and Saturn, not used to hearing me enraged, cower behind the cosy armchair.

"As I mentioned before, Princess, there is a wizard law as old as time itself. As guardians, we must not interfere with the worlds we protect. We cannot change destiny. What will be, will be. Just like the butterfly effect, each change made out of place can have immeasurable effects."

I try to calm down as my breath gets sharper; my eyebrows tighten as I try desperately to understand this law.

"Believe me, dear Princess, if I could have helped you I would have. But don't you see?" he pleaded. "You did it. But if I had come in to the world, just my being there may have changed everything."

I close my eyes and breathe through my nose as my fists clench. I know he is right. I really do! I just can't help but feel angry that no one helped me.

"You didn't need my help, Princess."

My eyes shoot open. Can he read my mind?

"What animal am I thinking of right now?" I demand.

"I can't read your mind, dear," he chuckles. "But I do know you very well, and pink unicorns are indeed very beautiful."

Darn it. He's right! I shake the unicorn from my mind.

"So why are you telling me this now? Won't telling me about the Megalo change my destiny?" My anger begins to loosen and fade.

"No, the Megalo comes from outside of your world," he answers. "It is not meant for your world, thus it is not part of your destiny. The outcome of all this is unknown. Although I must inform you again, the Wizard law states I am forbidden to intervene once he arrives and thus becomes part of your world. My job is solely to keep it out of this world."

I begin to understand, and I feel myself going pink, embarrassed that I had lost my temper.

"I'm sorry I got angry at you; that wasn't fair," I say sheepishly.

"It's OK to be angry," he tells me softly, not a hint of sadness or judgement in his voice. "Sometimes anger is very useful."

"No, it's not! I must be perfect! And I must be good!" I shout again, as the anger suddenly erupts once more. Tears sting my eyes as my emotions spill out. I bury my face in my hands as the old Wizard gently puts his arms around my shoulders. I hear Max whine and feel him pawing my legs, desperately trying to reach me.

"My dear, expressing anger is perfectly normal and doesn't make you any less 'good'." He strokes my hair as I cling to him, my silent tears falling down my face.

I leave the Wizard's embrace. Wiping my tears, I bend down to stroke Max's silky ears, his eyes large and round with concern.

I stand tall and take a deep breath. "I'm—"

"And don't apologize." The Wizard winks at me.

I smile meekly, still ashamed of my outburst.

"How much time do I have before the Megalo arrives?" I ask.

The Wizard's moustache twitches.

"We estimate just a few days."

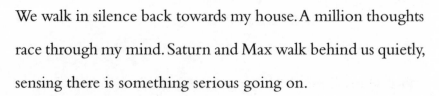

We walk in silence back towards my house. A million thoughts race through my mind. Saturn and Max walk behind us quietly, sensing there is something serious going on.

The Wizard stops upon reaching Grandfather Oak, and the two of them chat like old friends while I ponder my thoughts. I feel Grandfather Oak's eyes on me as the Wizard informs him of the new threat to our world, and how I must reach out to the Witch. I turn my back to them and walk over to the bridge, and stare down at the squids moving peacefully through the water. I'm just not in the mood to talk right now.

As the sun melts into evening, the Wizard turns to me.

"I must leave now, Princess, and do what I can to defend the entrance to your world. You must contact the Witch and work together. It's your only chance."

I nod my head as the Wizard reaches out and grabs hold of my hands. I squeeze back. "Thank you," I whisper.

The Wizard looks me in the eye. His eyes are not afraid any more. "I can't say exactly how long I will be away, battling the Megalo. It is my hope that I can come back in a few days and report that the threat is gone. But you must prepare for the worst possibility." With a loving smile, he disappears with a **pop**, leaving a faint breeze in his wake.

"Amy?" Grandfather Oak calls softly.

"Please, Grandfather, I just want to go up to my room and sleep," I say, and I turn my back to him once more as I enter my home, pull myself upstairs and fall into my bed. I feel more eyes on me as the other pups and cats look on, worried about what's going on. I'm sure Saturn and Max will fill them in, but for now … I just want to be alone. I pull the pillow over my head and close my eyes, embracing the darkness…

CHAPTER 5

"So, now you need my help, do ya, Princess?" snarls Captain Silverbeard. I avoid his eye and instead stare at the wooden deck beneath my boots. If you look real close, you can see the blue of the sea through the hairline cracks in the wood. I breathe deeply as I feel a cocktail of emotions: anger, humiliation, resentment and most of all guilt. Guilt for betraying myself and the people of Driftwood Bay.

I say nothing.

"I will help you, Princess."

I hear the crooked smile in his voice before I see it on his

face. I meet his eye finally. It's alive with a twisted glee as he sits in his giant, self-made throne, adorned with the skulls of his victims.

"Beg," he barks.

What choice do I have? I need his help, or Driftwood Bay will be invaded by the Pirates of the West! I close my eyes as

I lower my knees to the wooden deck. I take a deep breath through my nose, inhaling the salted sea air.

"Please," I say, through gritted teeth.

"You have to do better than that!" the Captain spits.

I glare at him. "Please," I say again.

I can see he is enjoying this a little too much. He taps his yellowed fingernails on a skull on the armrest of his throne.

"Certainly, sweet Princess." His smile sends shivers down

my spine. "When you give me the people of Driftwood Bay."

The words cut through me like a knife. I rise to my feet. "Never!" I scream, my face burning with anger. "I will never let them suffer! You can take me, but you will never have them!" I clench my fists and stomp my feet hard.

"That's the deal, Princess. Give them and the land to me, or kiss them all goodbye!"

He can't do this! I won't let him do this! I can't let Captain Silverbeard take it over; he will destroy the land and its people! He will destroy them! He will—

★★★

I wake up with a start, drenched in a cold sweat once again and my heart beating fast.

I sit up and hug my knees. The soft snoring and sleepy noises from my dogs bring some comfort in the otherwise silent night.

A longing I have never felt before takes me by surprise.

"I want my mother," I whisper.

★★★

I wake up earlier than I usually would. The sun has barely made it morning. The dogs are still fast asleep, but I smile when I see Boomer's leg twitch as he dreams. Romeo whimpers softly, no doubt talking to his dream squirrels. I gently climb over the dogs as if I'm playing a game of Twister, placing each hand and foot in any available space without waking them. I don't want to take a dog with me today. Not today. Today could be my day of reckoning.

I must find the Witch.

I hear shuffling from upstairs, coming from the attic. "What now?" I say to myself. I quietly make my way to the stairs and climb up, carefully avoiding the squeaky step. The attic is full of chests and boxes of old clothes and items I have found along my travels – as well as very thick cobwebs! I don't like coming up here.

I spot Mittens in a corner, his head buried in an old chest.

"Mittens, what are you doing?" I ask, folding my arms and tapping my foot.

He jumps with a start. Covered from head to toe in old jewellery and clothes, he looks very sheepish at being caught playing. A vintage copper-and-brass scuba helmet adorns his pumpkin head, while about a zillion necklaces of all shapes and sizes hang from his neck. And about seven different scarves, a large glossy handbag, fancy dinner gloves … as well as an old cooking apron and ballerina's tutu!

In spite of my dark mood, I can't help but giggle. "Oh Mittens, you are crazy!"

I laugh as he opens the little window of the scuba helmet and smiles his toothy pumpkin-head smile.

"Just don't make a mess, OK? Put all this stuff back when you're done."

I continue to hear him rummage as I climb the stairs back down.

I grab my backpack and fill it with food, supplies and, of course, Katniss. I quietly sneak out the front door. Bert and Bertha never sleep – they spend every second guarding the house from beasties – but I can hear their iron feet stomping on the carpet above, unaware, as I quietly close the front door.

The dew from last night holds on tightly to the blades of grass as I make my way towards the bridge. I tiptoe past Grandfather Oak, careful not to wake him. He breathes deeply in his slumber, a sleepy smile spread across his face as little birds fly around his branches.

I place my foot on the bridge and hear—

"Good morning, Amy."

I stop, my left foot hovering, just about to take another step.

"Good morning, Grandfather," I say timidly.

"Come here, dear," he says, his voice full of warmth and kindness.

I turn from the bridge and walk back to my tree. I feel too ashamed to look him in the eye, after ignoring him last night. I stare at my boots as the morning breeze sweeps through my hair.

Suddenly, I feel something grab my back and push me forward. I jump in shock and find Grandfather Oak's branch gently guiding me in for a hug. I wrap my arms around him and feel the roughness of his bark against my cheek, his earthy smell and the warm energy of his spirit. His branches hold me tight in an embrace that I have been longing for. A love that can only come from family. *I could stay here all day*, I think to myself.

But I can't. As I pull away and his branches retreat, I smile gratefully.

"Why didn't you come to me, Amy?" he asks.

I think deeply before I answer. The truth is, I'm not sure. "I guess I just need to face this on my own this time. I need to be strong and find myself. Find my strengths and face the darkness ... again."

"It's OK to be scared, Amy," Grandfather Oak replies.

"I don't want to be afraid any more. I don't want to be a kid.

I'm ready to grow up. I'm ready to see what monsters are out there. I'm ready to accept that the world isn't perfect. That bad things happen." I didn't take a single breath while I let out all that has built up inside me recently.

Grandfather Oak nods, his eyes full of understanding.

"I guess my whole life I have never really known who I am, where I come from. I've had no real childhood, no family. I've always just … been here. I learned to survive, and I am proud of that. But I can't let this … this Megalo monster thing end it all, everything I've built and achieved. And if that means begging the Witch for help, then I will do it."

"You have been thinking a lot about your past, haven't you?" Grandfather Oak asks.

"What past? I don't have one. All I remember is just being here. I have no memories. No family. Nothing but this land. And nothing is going to stop me from protecting it." My newfound strength surprises me.

"Of course you have a past, dear. I'm sure all will become clear one day." He smiles.

"How? I know … so little about myself, about life. What is it like to have a mother? To have a father?" I ask quietly, looking once again to the ground, to shield the pain that I know is showing in my eyes.

"My dear, all your questions will be answered in time," he replies.

I shake my head, forbidding the tears to fall.

"Amy, you are the bravest spirit I have ever been blessed with knowing. You have overcome challenges far bigger than yourself. One day, you will understand your past and make sense of it. It will come back to you, when you yourself are truly ready."

"If there is another day. Grandfather, this battle with the Megalo… How do I even find the Witch?" I ask, swallowing down the pain.

"The Witch is very well hidden, I am sure. She hasn't been seen since she cast the Darkness Hex. I would suggest listening to your instincts and following them. You are more powerful than you think, and magic – if you tune into it – can guide you."

Not the kind of answer I was hoping for, but I guess it will do.

"Thanks, Grandfather." I smile as I leave for the bridge once more.

"One more thing, Amy," he calls.

I stop and turn.

"Don't forget love and kindness will always win."

"I won't," I reply. And smile again, this time with more feeling. Strange: there is a sudden energy inside me. Like a shining light.

And the light is showing me the way I need to go.

CHAPTER 6

After hiking through the snowy forest, I welcome the humidity of the swamp. Although I shudder at the thought of my hair smelling like a toad!

I have never really travelled east of the Land of Love before. And I still don't really know where I am going. But something in me does, and I need to keep tuned in to that.

I spot an old, rotting boat tucked away under the fallen leaves of a giant swamp taro. After a few heaving attempts, I manage to pull it out to the murky green water, evicting a couple of turtles that had been resting on the bank.

"Sorry, guys," I say as I climb aboard. "But this is super important." Feeling guilty for disrupting them, I fish out the tomato slices from my sandwich and toss them to the turtles as a peace offering.

The turtles gratefully nibble at the food as I grab the heavy oars and start rowing.

The swamp offers a tranquil yet tense atmosphere. On one hand, it's so peaceful and lush in rich vegetation. But on the other, I feel watched by a million eyes. Dragonflies, frogs, toads, pond skaters, even alligators watch me as I glide past – and almost give me a heart attack when they nudge the boat.

I can hear flowing water, the chirping of crickets, the calls of frogs. I would love to come back some day and do some field research and get to know all these creatures better!

Suddenly, something knocks into the side of the boat so sharply that I drop my oar.

"Oh no!" I shriek as I watch it get swallowed up by the thick, soup-like swamp.

The boat gets knocked again, this time from the other side. I almost lose my balance! "What's going on?" I hold on the sides of the boat, breathing fast as all becomes still and quiet.

Too still and quiet. The noises have stopped. The chirping has stopped. The creatures have disappeared.

I gulp.

Suddenly, something large emerges from the swamp, just inches from the bow of my little boat. **An anaconda!**

It's a snake so big it could be bigger than Bertha standing on top of Bert with Mittens on top!

I fall, landing on my back in the damp boat as the anaconda snaps its huge jaws. It darts for me, but misses, its mouth too wide to fit in the boat.

I scream.

It darts for me again, and starts to bite away chunks of the hull in order to get to me. I have to think fast. I look overboard at the stinky, smoothie-like water.

"But my hair!" I moan.

I shake my head. My hair, or my life?

My decision made, I take a deep breath and dive into the green goo. I kick forward, splashing wildly, my feet stumbling across large roots. I manage to stand, but I can't stay still or my feet will sink into the muck.

The anaconda starts gaining on me as I wade, thrashing, across the thick swamp. I don't even have time to grab Katniss from my backpack; I just have to run. I grab a vine and pull myself out of the water, swinging on to drier land and run through the vegetation, hearing the anaconda not far behind, its jaws snapping away.

Then I trip on a tree root and fall to my knees. I turn to find the anaconda quickly encircling me, trapping me. The snake coils itself around my body, constricting me. I cannot move, I can barely breathe.

I literally feel the life being squeezed out of me. The more I struggle, the tighter the anaconda squeezes.

"Well, well, well. What have we here, then?" croaks a familiar voice.

I open my eyes.

Standing before me is none other than the Witch herself.

CHAPTER 7

"You have to help me!" I plead with the little energy that I have left as the snake tightens its hold on me.

"Really, Princess? Why on earth would I do that?" the Witch snorts.

"I need to tell you something. We are both in serious danger. Please!" I beg. My chest hurts now; my lungs are being deflated like old balloons.

"Well, you can just tell me now. Before you die!" Her eyes gleam with excitement as she folds her arms. She is clearly enjoying watching my untimely doom.

"I-I can't breathe. P-please!" Everything is beginning to go white. My head falls back, leaning on another coil of the anaconda. I feel the snake's tongue on my cheek as its head passes by.

The Witch sighs.

With a flick of her wand and a few weird words, the snake suddenly disappears in a cloud of purple smoke. I fall to the forest floor on my hands and knees with a thud.

"Thank you," I manage, massaging my throat and flicking away frog spawn from my hair. I try to stand up, but the Witch flicks her wand again and mutters another weird word, instructing vines from a nearby tree to circle my wrists and drag me up, restraining me. I pull on the vines, but it is no use.

"Now, talk," the Witch demands, standing before me with her eyebrows knotted in anger. She appears to be very disappointed having to delay my gruesome death.

"The Land of Love and everything in it is in danger, and I need your help," I say, looking into her deep purple eyes.

Her cackle cuts through me like glass.

"Please, you don't understand!" I beg, pulling my weight down on the vines in frustration. "Without you, we are all doomed! That includes you! And your ... precious beasties."

I feel something warm on my head; my tiara's jewel is glowing bright, its light reflecting in the eyes of the Witch.

She stops laughing suddenly, her top lip curling as she stares at me.

I explain everything the old Wizard told me. I explain about the Megalo and how the only thing that could possibly stop him is magic.

"Why should I believe you?" she hisses.

"I … I don't know. But you have to," I say. "Neither of us is strong enough to defeat this creature alone. We both need to fight him. And I've only cast one spell before, so I don't know how to fight. I need you to teach me how to work magic, and together we'll stop him from destroying everything we love."

The Witch falls silent, pondering my words. I wait, watching her as she paces in front of me.

"Fine. But I am not doing this for you. I'm doing it for me and my beasties. I'm not afraid of this … this *Megalo*." She stands in front of me, her eyes narrowing. "But I want payment."

"Payment?"

"I want your tiara, Princess."

My tiara? No way! "But I can't!" I plead.

"That's the deal, child, take it or leave it." She folds her arms and turns her back to me.

Why does she want my tiara? I wonder. I can't let her have it; the tiara is one of the only clues I have about my family, about my past.

But I need her help. I need the Witch. I close my eyes and take a deep breath.

"OK," I say. "But only once the Megalo is defeated. Only then can you have it."

Sadness fills my heart at the thought of losing the one piece of my origins. But for the greater good, I must give it up.

The Witch turns to me, a wicked smile across her haggard face. "Splendid. Meet me tomorrow at dusk in the birch forest for your first lesson."

"Thank you so—"

"Shut up," she spits, then turns to leave.

"Erm, one more thing?" I ask.

"What?" the Witch snaps, turning back.

"Erm…Think you could let me down?" I ask sheepishly.

She sighs, and – with another wave of her wand – the vines release me and I fall to the ground.

Ow.

CHAPTER 8

I am bombarded by nine very anxious dogs as I walk into my house. Their cries and whines drown out the heavy footsteps of Bert and Bertha, whose faces also look a mix between anger and relief.

"I'm sorry I worried you, guys," I say as I try to comfort them. Mars holds my hand in his mouth as Luna licks my knees. Max and Sailor wrestle each other, trying to jump up into my arms, as Destiny tells off my boots for letting me go outside without her.

I smell my hair. "Urgh, swamp juice!" I gag.

After a hot bubble bath and shampooing my hair about a zillion times until it finally smells normal – like creamy coconut – I put on my comfy dressing gown and feed the dogs and cats, who are now much more relaxed. Then I take a cup of hot chocolate out to the balcony. I sit and hug my knees close under the blanket of stars. The moon paints my Land of Love in its magical silver glow.

I sip my drink and feel the velvety chocolate warm my body. I look to the stars, wondering where the exit to leave this world is, to go to the next. I imagine a long corridor of thousands of doors, each one opening up to the stars of a different world.

If I squint, it looks like the stars are dancing. Twirling and spinning around.

72

I feel very alone. A single tear falls from my eye as I watch the stars.

Then I suddenly feel an icy chill on my shoulders. I turn to find Mittens, his arm wrapped around me, and he holds me close. Still wearing his silly necklaces and scuba helmet. I shake with the chill, and my tear freezes on my cheek as I squeeze his icy tummy.

My crazy Mittens, how I love him!

★★★

"What are those rats doing here?" snarls the Witch, glaring over my shoulder. I turn to find each of my nine dogs lined up, teeth baring, growling and ready to attack.

"Hush, puppies!" I whisper loudly to them. Then I turn back to face the Witch. "Sorry, they wouldn't let me meet you alone. They wanted to make sure that I was safe."

"Pfft!" The Witch rolls her eyes and straightens her purple pointed hat over her knotted, seaweed-like hair. "Let's just get this over with."

She paces in front of me, her long robes dragging on the forest floor. Then she pulls out her wand.

"Grrrrrrrrrrrrr!" Mars pounces ahead of the others, his eyes alive with anger. He remembers the last time he saw the Witch use her wand – he almost died!

The Witch sticks her tongue out at him, which sets the whole pack into a barking frenzy.

"Dogs! I order you to be quiet!" I shout, and they reluctantly retreat, growling softly.

"I'm going to teach you some of darkest magic passed down from the Witch Elders," the Witch says. "This first spell lets me manipulate nearby objects."

She raises her wand, pointing it at a nearby tree. **"IMPERIUM!"** she shouts.

A jet of purple lightning shoots from her wand and hits the tree. It suddenly comes to life, shaking from its top to its roots, its branches dancing in the air, mirroring the movement of her wand. The Witch cackles as she makes the tree dance. The thick trunk is thrown forward, hitting the ground with a mighty *thump*. It hits the ground again, and again, and again. I can feel it under my feet, the earth shaking with each thud.

"Stop! You're hurting him!" I scream, my heart beating fast. That poor tree!

"Oh, please," she spits as she flicks her wand again, ending the spell.

I run over to the tree and place my hand upon its trunk.

The warm energy I should feel there is cold. I stroke the rough bark and close my eyes, imagining transferring my own energy into the tree.

Slowly, the bark beneath my hand warms up, and it isn't long before the tree is once again full of spirit.

"Your turn," the Witch says. She smiles menacingly as she holds out her wand to me.

I stare at the twisted piece of black hawthorn wood in her hand, and I shudder at the misery it has caused. The damage it has done. I don't even want to touch it.

But then I realize: it's not the wand. It's the Witch. She casts the spells; the wand is but a tool used for her wicked ways.

I reluctantly take the wand and notice how light it feels. How it almost feels like an extension of my arm. It feels so natural and ... *normal*.

"IMPERIUM!" I shout as I point the wand to the same tree. A soft pink whisper of smoke flows through the tip of the

wand like a stream, expanding as it reaches the tree, engulfing it in a pearly cloud, and the tree once again comes to life. I aim the wand towards the longest branch and giggle as I make it wave at the dogs.

Luna, who loves nature just as much as I do, skips over for a closer look. I make the branch gently pat Luna on her head as she wags her tail. I flick the wand, finishing the spell, and watch as the pink smoke fades away. A butterfly floats by Luna, who playfully runs after it.

The Witch snatches her wand back. "That was gross," she snarls. "OK, this next one lets me freeze anything I want. Watch!" Suddenly, she points the wand at my chest.

"No, wait!" I squeal.

"DURATIUS!" she shouts. Within seconds, I am unable to move, frozen like a statue. I can feel my heart beating against my chest, and feel the blood flow through my veins. My eyes can't move; they are frozen in a stare, fixated on the tip of the

Witch's wand. I try to move with all my might, but it's useless. I watch as the Witch flicks her wand again, and suddenly I fall to the ground. Every inch of my body fills with pins and needles.

The Witch cackles. "Now, you try it."

I stand up and take her wand once more. I point it towards the Witch.

"Not me, you silly girl!" she cries, cowering behind her arm. "One of the dogs!"

"What? No way," I say. "You're wasting time," the Witch says, snatching the wand back. An evil grin spreads over the Witch's yellowed teeth. "Now, **IMPERIUM!**" she screeches, pointing her wand at Luna's butterfly friend.

The butterfly dips and soars as the Witch takes control of it. Then it floats over to the river nearby, Luna following close behind.

"Luna! Stop!" I shout. But she can't hear me, she is transfixed

on the butterfly and is headed straight for the raging rapids! "Luna!"

Without a second thought, I snatch the wand from the Witch's hand. **"DURATIUS!"** I scream. The pink smoky trail flows from the wand and swallows Luna just as she slips from on the bank and tumbles towards the water. She is suspended in mid-air, her paws outstretched before her, a look of fear painted on her face.

"Yes!" I shout as I run over to her and pluck her from the air. She is so stiff! As I flick the wand to end the spell, I feel her body become soft and flexible again. She kisses my cheek as the other dogs run to us, yelping with all the excitement.

I lower Luna to the ground as the Witch walks over. She snatches the wand back from me again and growls.

"Urgh, you are so much like…" The Witch stops herself.

"Like who?" I ask.

The Witch turns away. "No one. Now, let's try another."

★★★

I fall into my bed, with every bone aching. Who knew learning magic would be so tiring? All those flicks and swooshes, all the jumping and twirling. My wand arm feels like an elephant has been dancing on it. And dancing badly.

Bert brings me some warm soup, which I am very grateful for … even though half of it ends up on the carpet, with his stumbling.

"Thanks, Bert!" I say, as I painfully stir the remaining soup. I watch as he picks up Boomer, who has fallen off the bed.

I suddenly have an idea. What if I teach Bert and Bertha all the magic I am learning? That way, we would have a small

army of magic to defeat the Megalo, not just the Witch and me! I could even train up the snow golems!

I'll see what the Witch thinks tomorrow, but right now, I need to rest.

CHAPTER 9

"Absolutely not. Magic cannot be taught. You either have it in you or you don't."

The Witch doesn't seem very excited about my magical army idea.

The early morning sun rises on the horizon as we head back to the forest, beams of light shooting through the gaps in the trees. I struggle to keep up with the Witch; she walks very fast, almost gliding along.

After yesterday's near-miss at the river, I made the dogs stay at home today.

"But you're teaching me!" I say, running out of breath.

The Witch stops walking and turns to me sharply, and I stop just in time to avoid stumbling into her, her nose only inches from my own and her eyes boring into mine.

"Enough!" she snarls. "I don't have time for your rubbish. Either shut up or go home."

I gulp. "OK," I say, my voice wobbling. She sure is scary.

The Witch turns, her thick, knotted hair slapping me in the face, and she speeds on ahead. I follow, trying hard to keep up.

Soon we are deep in the woods. The branches above entwine with each other, blocking out the sky. I find myself shivering as the Witch leads me to a small clearing, where the trees form a wall around us.

"OK, little vermin child, today I'm going to show you how to block curses." She paces in front of me, her wand gripped tightly in her bony hand.

A morning breeze floats through the trees and strokes my hair, leaving goosebumps on my skin. I sit on a fallen tree, the bark coated in damp moss.

The Witch stands before me and in her hands are two wands. One wand – her usual one – is black, dark and jagged. The other is a soft evergreen colour. It's jagged too, yet smooth. Not sharp.

"Take it," she whispers.

I gently grasp the green wand, and energy surges through my body, leaving every inch of my skin tingling. The wand feels warm in my hand. It becomes an extra finger, an extra hand or limb. It just fits. It belongs.

"Wow," I whisper, breathless. "Where did this come from?"

The Witch avoids my eyes. "I ... uh ... I found it."

"Found it where?" I ask as I turn the wand in my hand, fascinated.

"What have I told you about asking questions?" the Witch snaps.

I bite my lip and flick the wand playfully.

"And stop that!" she shouts. "Never flick or point a wand at someone unless you mean them harm!"

"But you're pointing your wand at me!"

"I know," she snarls, her eyes sparkling

"Oh."

I look for something to distract her. "Er … so … um… What do you want to teach me today?"

She breaks that awful stare and heads to the middle of the clearing. "Let's start with a simple protection bubble."

This is going to be a long day, I can already tell.

★★★

The Witch points her wand at me and, with a twisted smile, she shouts out her spell. A thick, black smog erupts from the tip of her wand and races towards me. I have mere seconds before that smog will burn through me like acid.

I draw my wand back, and with an almighty flick of the wrist I shout, **"INNOXIAS!"**

A cascade of pink flows from my wand and reaches the black smog. The two forces battle with each other, like huge waves of an angry sea. Each force trying to devour the other.

I feel my heart beating fast as my fist grips the wand so tightly it shakes.

I glance at the Witch, who looks just as tense as I feel. The black smog takes the form of a giant spider, its smoky legs trying to squeeze the life out of my force.

I close my eyes and imagine myself as a brave tiger, each stripe a medal of bravery. As I open my eyes, the pink smoke transforms into a tiger, its giant paws swiping at the spider.

The spider and tiger battle. The spider stretches out its eight legs to bind the tiger, but it isn't quick enough.

The pink tiger pounces on the arachnid's back with a mighty roar. The spider crumbles and falls to the floor, disappearing in a cloud of purple smoke. The tiger stands tall and bows his head to me before evaporating in the wind.

The forest falls into an eerie, post-battle silence, and I am speechless. After many hours of trial and error, I have finally stopped the Witch's spell.

"You did it," she whispers.

I look over and see she is … smiling!

"You really did it." She meets my eyes, and for a few seconds we share a rare mutual happiness. That is, until she remembers herself and scowls, then spits green goo on the floor. "Took you long enough, you useless swine."

I say nothing, but smile proudly.

"Even your mother learned that fas—"

"What?" I gasp, dropping the wand. "You knew my mother?!"

The Witch's eyes grow large. "I... Er..." she stutters.

I march over to her. "Tell me the truth!" I demand.

The Witch hesitates and turns to walk off, but I block her way by slamming my hand on the tree, over her shoulder.

"Now!" I order, my heart pounding.

The Witch raises an eyebrow for a moment, considering. Then she growls, "Fine. But not here. Meet me at the Alpine Mountains."

Suddenly, she disappears with a loud **pop**.

And I am left alone with my racing thoughts. She knew my mother? I can't believe it!

I turn to leave, but I notice the Witch's spare wand laying in the tall grass where I had dropped it. I walk over and pick it up, slipping it in my backpack. As afternoon falls into twilight, I make my way towards the mountains.

★★★

It's a long trek from the East Forest, but I am determined. After many hours of trudging onwards, I finally reach the rising rocks and boulders where the Alpine Mountains begin. I look up but fail to see the snowcapped tops; instead, the mountainside disappears into the twilit clouds above.

"You made it."

"Ahhh!" The Witch's voice behind me makes me jump. "So … er … are we going to your new secret mountain lair?" I ask.

"One of them."

She flicks her wand and mumbles something weird at a large boulder, which suddenly splits in two with a great noise like the sound of thunder. It reveals a stone staircase leading down into the mountain. The Witch leads the way.

The boulder closes behind us and the stairs are cloaked in darkness. As my heart races, my breath tries to keep up. I feel nervous. Scared. The butterflies are once again wrestling with each other in my tummy.

I am afraid, but not of the Witch. I am afraid of what she is going to tell me. I have wondered my whole life about my family, and now I will finally learn the truth.

"Lucidos," the Witch says, and the tip of her wand burns bright, lighting our way. A cold, earthy wind whisks past my cheeks. Each dusty step we take is mirrored in echoes, and our shadows bounce along down the stairs with us.

We reach the bottom, where a large, wooden, cobwebby door awaits us. The Witch once again flicks her wand and mutters some more gobbledegook, and the door creaks open.

I follow her into a large stone room, and the door slams shut behind us. The room is cold, but the Witch soon lights a fireplace, and it fills the room with a warm orange glow. I rub my hands together over the fire as my eyes explore the Witch's lair.

This is very different from the last lair I visited. The one where she held me captive and tried to kill me by feeding me to her spiders… But let's not think about that.

This room is rather cosy. Almost home-like… Well, for a witch, that is.

There is an old, moth-eaten grey sofa, and an armchair that smells slightly of mould is positioned in front of the fireplace. Old tin cans with black roses and weeds adorn the mantelpiece. Large bookcases filled with large leather books of all sizes stand proudly against the stone walls, and uneven, slanted shelving

units display the weirdest things – a three-headed mouse skull,
a jar filled with liquid gold, petrified unicorn poop, fossilized
fairy wings and leprechaun hair trimmings in a crystal jar.

A wooden picture frame sits on the top shelf, cobwebs
sprouting from the top corners. Curious, I stand on tiptoe,

trying to see the photo, but dust coats the picture so much that I can't make anything out. I pull the frame from the shelf and am just about to blow the dust off when—

"Get your filthy little hands off that, you little twerp!"

"I-I'm sorry," I mumble.

The Witch glares at me.

"So ... erm ... you knew my mother?" I ask.

The Witch looks uncomfortable as she slams the picture frame down on the mantelpiece. "Yes... I knew her," she answers.

"Can you tell me about her?" I ask as I carefully sit on the mouldy sofa.

The Witch stands in front of the fireplace and stares down into the roaring fire, the flames dancing with every spit and crackle. After what seems like an eternity, she finally turns to me.

"She was my sister."

CHAPTER 10

I laugh out loud.

"Ha! That's funny! It almost sounded like you said my mother was your sister! Ha! Ha! Too funny." I wipe my eyes with my hand, giggling at the very thought of it.

The Witch stands watching me, glowering.

"I'm sorry, I'm sorry," I giggle. "You were saying?"

"It's true," the Witches growls.

I begin to giggle again. Who knew the Witch could be such a joker? If she weren't so psychotic, she and Mittens would get on really well!

"Stop laughing!" the Witch roars, slamming her hands on the mouldy sofa either side of me. I shriek and lean back, my eyes wide in fright.

"Sorry!" I squeak.

The Witch stands tall once again and picks up the picture frame from the mantelpiece. Using her cloak sleeve, she wipes the dust from the photo before passing it to me.

Staring up at me are two little girls, one giving a piggyback ride to the other. The girl giving the piggyback looks to be maybe nine or ten years old. The other girl looks around six or seven. The older girl is laughing, her wavy purple hair bouncing around her face. The younger girl is overjoyed, her eyes closed in delight as she clings to her big

sister. Her pink hair is in bunches, hanging beside her ears. She looks like … like me! A little me.

I realize I am not breathing and draw in a sharp, staggered breath.

"You're saying … this is my mother," I whisper as I stroke the pink hair through the glass.

The Witch nods.

"And this is you?" I look up to the Witch and see the wavy-haired little girl's eyes glowering back at me. The little freckle on the girl's nose is now a big, hairy wart.

"Yes," she answers.

Everything goes numb. My fingers, my toes. I feel dizzy. As I glance at the fireplace, the flames dance slowly, and the only sounds I can hear are my own shallow breaths. A billion thoughts race through my mind. If the Witch really is my mother's sister, then that means…

"You're my aunt?"

The witch's worm–like lips quiver. "Yes."

I stand up on trembling legs, the photo frame falling to the floor. The glass cracks, a perfect line dividing the two sisters.

This can't be real! I pace the length of the room, my hands massaging my head. This has got to be a joke. Or a trick.

"Where is my mother now? And my father?" I ask.

The Witch physically shudders at the mention of my father. "They're dead."

An hour ago, I didn't have a family, I didn't have a past. And now, I have lost everything I have always wanted, but never had. How is any of this possible?

I glare at the Witch, my confusion and anger aimed at her.

"You were bound to find out sometime," she says, sinking into her mouldy armchair.

"I want to know everything," I say, sitting on the sofa.

The Witch sighs. "Your father and I were madly in love."

"Ew, gross!" Did I just say that out loud? I slam my hand

across my mouth, shocked at my own outburst. "Sorry," I mumble.

The Witch glares at me, saying nothing, her hands curled up in her fists, which are now shaking with anger … or rage … her eyes almost popping out of her sockets…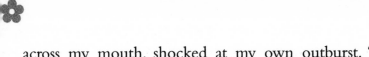

"Erm … so what happened?" I ask, hoping to distract her from killing me right there and then.

The Witch takes a deep breath. "As I was saying," she hisses, "your father and I were in love. Until your mother ruined everything, that is. I could see it in their eyes, that sparkle he once had for me. It broke my heart. THEY broke my heart. And she stole my life."

The Witch looks into the burning fire. Perhaps to hide her pain.

Then she continues, "Your father was a prince. And I would have been a princess. Once his father died, we would have ruled the land together."

The Witch suddenly stands, her body trembling with rage. "But your mother took all that away from ME!" she shouts, the fire's flames reflected in her eyes. "My own sister. I hated her. I hated him. She was always the pretty one, the good one. Her magic was always perfect, always—"

"Magic?" I interrupt. "She was a … a…"

"A witch, yes," the Witch answers impatiently, then adds in disgust, "a White Witch. Of course she would have the Magic of the Angels. Oh, Mum and Dad were so proud of their little White Witch, whereas I was nothing special, or so they thought."

She catches sight of my face and sniggers. "Close your mouth! You're not a frog catching flies, are you? Disgusting child."

I promptly shut my mouth, which had been hanging open in disbelief.

"After their awful wedding, and being crowned the new king and queen, they had you." Her left eye begins twitching. "And what a perfect family you were. But no one cared about me, did they? She took my life! MY LIFE!"

The Witch bangs her fist down on the mantelpiece, making the black petals fall from her midnight roses. Her anger echoes through the stone room, vibrating from the floor to the ceiling. "Well, what happens next? I run off to the wilderness, where – long story short – I make friends."

"Friends?"

"The Elder Witches. They were the only ones who cared about me, who saw my potential. They taught me ancient magic – dark, powerful magic. I became the Witch I was always meant to be…" She drifts off, smiling at a memory.

"But my parents?"

"Right, them. Well, tragedy struck. Or justice, in my view. My scheming little sister and her vile husband were killed in an accident. They were riding horses when a storm came. A bolt of lightning spooked the horses, which caused your parents to fall to their deaths."

Tears spring to my eyes. Tears for my unknown parents.

Then I think of all the times I have seen the Witch control the weather, create storms, and anger flares within me. "Did you kill them?"

"No," she replies, indignant. "I did not. But of course with them gone, the land now belonged to you. If only something terrible were to happen to you too, then the land would be mine! So I admit, I did cast a spell, one that wiped your memory. I had plans to get rid of you, but before I could, you disappeared. And, years later, you suddenly returned. That was the day you took the land back from me. My curse on you only lasted until you came of age, so I now have no choice

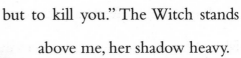

but to kill you." The Witch stands above me, her shadow heavy.

I stand up on wobbly legs. Is she threatening me? I have to get out of here! I grab my backpack and make a run for the door. It's locked! I rattle the round iron handle and pound the heavy wood with my fists. I hear the Witch walking towards me, her cloak dragging on the dusty floor. My heart starts to beat faster. She's getting closer. I pull the handle with all my might, but it's useless. The Witch looks down at me, expressionless.

Is she going to kill me?

She reaches for her wand as I back up and slide away, along the cold stone wall.

She points it at me. I put my arms up, covering my face.

"Natantisio," she commands.

My backpack suddenly comes to life, wriggling and jumping on my back as if there is a monkey in there. I can feel the zipper being pulled and watch as the evergreen wand floats towards the witch's open hand.

Uh-oh.

"I was bringing it back to you!" I plead. "Honest!"

The Witch holds out the wand to me. **"Apertus,"** she whispers and nods towards the door.

She's letting me go?

Confused, I take the wand in my shaking hand and head towards the door. I flick the wand and repeat the spell. The door swings open and I am greeted by a cold, dusty wind.

"That wand was your mother's," the Witch says.

I turn back to her, but I can't take my eyes of the wooden stick in my hand.

"Keep it. Tomorrow the lessons continue in the East Forest," she says.

I don't know what to say. My head feels like it's going to explode.

I say nothing, and instead run up the cold stone stairs. As I reach the large boulder at the top, I shout, **"Apertus!"**

It swings open, revealing a downpour of rain. I don't even care about my hair. I just want to go home and be with my dogs. I run for home, the rain camouflaging my tears as I cradle my mother's wand in my arms.

CHAPTER 11

I don't want to wake up.

I feel myself being pulled from my dream as the other side of my brain wakes up and reality seeps in. I grumble. My eyes slowly open and begin to focus on a man with a big bushy beard STARING DOWN AT ME.

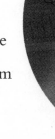

"Arrrrrgh!!!!!" I scream.

"I'm so sorry, Princess!" the Wizard says, leaping up from

where he was sitting at the end of my bed. "I didn't mean to startle you!" The dogs all wake in a frenzy, and Mittens marches in, armed with a snowball aimed right for the Wizard's head.

"No, Mittens, don't! It's OK!" I assure him. Mittens looks at me and lowers his ammunition. He readjusts his necklaces and tutu, and closes the window of his scuba helmet with a slam. "Good boy," I say.

Boomer struggles to stay awake and flops on to the carpet, snoring, while Mittens shows off his necklaces and medallions to Sailor.

I turn to the Wizard and try to get my breath back. "What are you doing here?" I ask.

"The Megalo is getting closer, Princess. He destroyed another dimension that is only a few light-years away from yours."

I feel the fear in the pit of my stomach start to grow.

But Luna's sleepy yawn is a cute distraction from our impending doom. I sit back on my bed and pull her into my arms. She snuggles in to the nook in my elbow as her tail wags, hitting Max in the face – who doesn't look too impressed.

"I met the Witch. She's been teaching me magic," I tell the Wizard.

"I know, dear, I have been watching," he answers.

I stroke Luna's silky ears as Lola joins us and snuggles on my lap too. "Can I ask you something?"

"Of course, Princess."

"Why didn't you tell me? About my family, about my past. You must have known." I must admit, I feel a little resentful towards the kind Wizard.

"Well, as guardian it is my duty to be fully aware of everything that happens in the worlds I protect. But I don't know what will happen when something breaks our laws, such as a Megalo. He doesn't belong here, so he has no place in your destiny. So it is my duty to warn you, to protect the world. But I am forbidden from telling you things about the past that could affect your future. As I told you before, one tiny change can alter your entire world. Remember how a single flutter of a butterfly's wing could, possibly, change everything? Well, the Megalo is the butterfly. And telling you about your past could be another butterfly."

I nod, my resentment fading. It makes sense, I just don't want it to. I want to find a way out … someone to blame.

"What does the Megalo do, when it attacks a world?"

"It sucks power through its mouth. It emits a beam of light that draws the power from the land, draining the world until it is nothing but a barren shell … if even that." He shakes his head sadly.

"So we need to cut off its head?" I ask, thinking of my diamond sword.

"No, we guardians tried that already. The head can grow back in an instant."

I think for a moment. "Before you said that dark magic works against it. Why don't you guys learn to fight with that?"

"You can't just learn dark magic, Princess. Magic is part of who and what you are. You are born into the art, good or bad."

I suddenly remember what the Witch said before, when I mentioned teaching Bert and Bertha magic: you can't teach magic. You either have it in you, or you don't.

"Wait a minute… My mother was a witch, a White Witch. And the Witch is my aunt…" – I shudder – "and she's a Black Witch. Does that mean … I'm a witch?" My eyes widen at the sudden query. I look to the Wizard, who promptly stands up.

"I must be off, Princess! I shall do whatever I can to protect you and your world."

And he disappears with a **pop**.

"No way!" I whisper to myself. Luna and Lola look up at me with sleepy eyes.

I'm a witch?

CHAPTER 12

After feeding the dogs and cats, and reassuring them that even though I'm not taking them with me, I love them all dearly and I'm going to be safe, I set off to meet the Witch in the East Forest.

My mother's wand in my backpack feels like it's weighing me down. I have so many questions about the wand, about myself. And only one person can answer them.

I reach the meadow that lies in the middle of the four forests. To the left of me is the West Forest, where the Witch had unleashed the Darkness Hex. The long meadow grass poking

my knees and the blackbirds flying around the treetops bring

back memories of that dreaded curse.

"Rrruff!"

I turn around to find a bundle of fluff leaping through the

long grass. "Mars?"

Mars jumps up at me, wagging his tail. "What are you doing

here? I told you to stay home!" I bend down and stroke him

under his chin, his favourite spot. "Couldn't resist an adventure, huh?" Mars barks playfully and headbutts my knee.

I stand and look over my beautiful soldier trees, the first ones to be eaten by the Hex. They now stand tall and thriving, not the empty shells they once were.

Turning, I head into the East Forest with Mars at my side. Golden, brittle leaves crunch beneath our boots and paws as autumn blankets the ground.

Eventually I see the Witch in the distance, through the oak trees. I stop and watch her for a few minutes, fascinated. I feel angry at her, yet also somewhere deep down I feel pity.

I shake my head. Now is not the time to feel. I want more answers. I walk with confidence through to the clearing, where the Witch is collecting feathers and berries.

"Am I a witch?" I ask, stopping just behind her.

"No 'good morning', then?" She stuffs a bunch of white feathers in a little black pouch. The fallen leaves cling to the bottom of the Witch's cloak as she shuffles around collecting her trinkets.

Mars barks to alert the Witch that he is here with me and that she better not be mean or she will have to answer to him.

The Witch rolls her eyes and sticks out her green tongue at him. Mars growls, and I use my boot to hold him back from lunging at her.

"Well?" I ask.

The Witch sighs. "Yes. Yes, you are. Although your father was mortal, a daughter of a witch has a high chance of being a witch as well. I always had my suspicions, but I did not know for sure until you broke my Darkness Hex."

I sit on a fallen oak log to digest this new information, careful not to disturb the growing fungus. Mars lays his head on my knee. "Why do you hate me?" I ask.

The Witch hastily plucks the fungus from the log and stuffs it in her pouch. "Simple. Because you're gross."

"That's not really a reason," I reply softly. "You … you're my family. My aunt."

Aunt.

The Witch is MY AUNT.

Auntie Witch? I shake my head at the thought. This is all too weird.

"I hate you because I can. After we defeat this Megalo I will kill you and take this land back. Now, get up!"

★★★

"Dimissio!" I shout, pointing my wand at her.

The Witch's wand suddenly flies from her grip and comes at me with incredible speed. I catch it with my free hand – and wince as my fingers throb in pain.

"Ow!!" I cry.

"Don't be such a baby. They're not broken, are they?" the Witch says, snatching her wand back. I shake my hand out, which makes the pain even worse.

"Sure does feel like it," I say, even though I can see my fingers are fine.

It's dark now, but after spending all day training, I have learned how to disarm an enemy. I'm not sure if the Megalo will have a wand, or a big scary axe, or a laser gun that shoots radioactive mutant bumblebees, but it's a useful spell to know.

Suddenly, thunder erupts. It's so loud, I cover my ears in fright. It rumbles through the dark sky, down to the earth, vibrating the ground beneath us. Then lightning strikes, illuminating the forest. The Witch slowly walks ahead of me, looking up as a soft wind whisks past us.

Mars cowers behind my legs, trembling.

"We better go before the rain comes," I say, scooping up my

dog. "Plus I used this really rare stuff on my hair this morning, just before I straightened it, so I really don't want to get it wet. It might go all frizzy! And I hate it when it goes frizzy becau—"

"This is not a storm, Princess," the Witch interrupts, her voice calm. "The lightning should come before the thunder, not the other way around."

I look up to the sky, bordered by the tops of the trees. There are no stars, just a vast, black emptiness.

"The stars are in hiding," she adds, chilling me to the bone.

I stand beside her, squeezing a quivering Mars as the thunder makes me jump once more. Goose bumps spread over my skin, and I can feel my pulse beat faster.

"The Megalo is here."

CHAPTER 13

"What do we do?" I cry. I grab the Witch's hand in panic.

"Urgh, don't touch me," she snarls, shaking me off and wiping her hand on her cloak.

Thunder roars again.

"Look!" the Witch shouts, pointing a bony white finger.

Lightning rips through the sky … but it doesn't disappear. It stays there, painted above us. A giant, glowing white zigzag.

"It's … moving," I whisper, watching as the lightning

bolt appears to stretch and pulse, as if something is behind it, prodding it.

Suddenly, the bolt widens and a large black shape emerges from it. It's a crack! The lightning bolt is a crack!

"It's breaking through the sky," the Witch says in disbelief.

I stand open-mouthed as what looks to be a black claw grasps at the sides of the widening fissure in the sky and pulls,

forming hundreds of more lightning cracks and snapping away giant chunks of the night sky. It's as if my world is an egg, and its shell is being peeled away.

"Princess!"

"Arrrggh!" I scream as the old Wizard materializes in front of me.

"You have to stop doing that!" I say, catching my breath and picking up Mars, whom I dropped in fright. I kiss his head, and he forgives me.

"I'm sorry, Princess! But I must warn you, the Megalo"– he takes a deep breath – "is on its way."

"You're a bit late, old man," the Witch says bitterly, and points to the sky.

The Wizard turns and looks up, pushing his glasses up his nose.

"Oh my!" he says.

We stand together and watch as more of the creature squeezes through the lightning bolt.

"How big is it?" I ask, watching as more and more of it just keeps on coming.

"We estimate it being around half the size of a Trunkatusky."

"Trunkatusky?" I ask, confused.

"Oh yes! Wrong dimension! Erm, OK, in your world … about forty African elephants."

I gulp.

"Wait, forty elephants is only half the size of the trunkythingy? What does it look like?" I am so intrigued about this whimsical-sounding beast…

"Now's not the time, Princess! We really must hurry!"

I shake my head. I must be focused. *Right, let's get everyone to a safe place,* I think.

"We have to hide the animals!" I say. "Oh! I have a bunker

deep under my house! It's got survival gear, beds, food… They will all be super safe there!"

"Perfect," he says. "But I must return to the fight now. I will do what I can, but if the Megalo fully breaches your world, I cannot help you any more."

"I know." I nod. I understand the Wizard is not allowed to help in the battles of the worlds he cares for.

I turn to him. "Thank you for everything." I try to smile.

The Wizard embraces me. I hold him tight and take in his smell of shortbread biscuits, English tea and the faint musky smell of frankincense.

He lets go and holds my shoulders at arm's length. His milky blue eyes fill with tears while he smiles a wobbly smile.

"Thank you for helping Amy," he says to the Witch, holding out a hand for her to shake.

"Pfft! I'm not helping her. By rights, this is *my* world, and after I've saved it from that thing I will take it back." She folds her arms and turns her back on the Wizard's hand.

"Yes … er … well. Good luck to the both of you. Work together and look after each other." And with a final shaky smile, the Wizard disappears with a **pop**.

"OK, let's hurry," I say to the Witch. But as I turn to leave the forest, and she too disappears with a **pop**!

Why didn't she teach me that spell? I wonder as a leaf caught in the wind hits me in the face.

★★★

"OK, guys, we gotta get you in hiding!" I address my family, who have all gathered in the living room, alert and anxious. Together, we head towards the library. With the touch of a hidden button, two bookshelves pull apart, revealing a secret stairway.

I lead the way, followed by Bert and Bertha, Mittens, Mr Frost and Blizzard, nine dogs, three cats, three horses, one donkey, one pig, and finally one chicken bringing up the rear. It takes a long time to reach the bunker, climbing down about a zillion stairs, until I wonder whether we have reached the earth's core.

But soon the animals are all settled in, testing out the bounciness of the beds.

Three loud bangs on the iron door make me jump. Surely the Megalo wouldn't knock?

"Who's there?" I ask, trying to keep my voice steady.

"Let me in, you silly girl, or I'll huff and I'll puff and I'll blow this house until it's nothing but splinters and dust bunnies."

I gulp as I pull open the heavy door, and there stands the

Witch, surrounded by her precious beasties. Spiders larger than cars, skeletons armed with bows and arrows, ogres that have destroyed my stairs with their big ol' feet, and other scary and strange-looking creatures.

I suddenly feel Bert's big iron arm pull me away as he and Bertha confront the beasties. The Witch points her wand at them threateningly.

"Wait!!" I shout, jumping back in between them.

"My family must be safe too," the Witch says.

And for a brief second, in her eyes I see desperation. I look at her strange family of creatures. They are monsters and beasts, but she is right. Her family deserve to be safe.

"OK, OK. Bert, lift me up."

Bert picks me up so swiftly I must weigh like a feather to him. I stand on his shoulders.

"Everybody, listen up!" I shout, cupping my hands around

my mouth. The cats stop purring, the dogs stop growling at the beasties, the horses stop stomping their hooves. The only sound is of melting snowballs dripping on my floor; my snow golems each have one aimed at the newcomers.

"The Witch I and have called a truce!" I announce.

"*Temporary* truce," the Witch corrects me, stroking the hairy leg of one of her giant spiders, who has his leg wrapped his leg around her protectively.

"Right, temporary truce. My family, I expect you to treat our guests with kindness. And … er … beasties … I expect you guys to not harm my family. Today, we are one. Today we come together to overcome something much bigger than all of us. Are we in agreement?"

I look to my family who all nod their heads. The beasties nod theirs too.

"Alrighty, then. Let's shake on it."

The spiders crawl forward, meeting the dogs, who shake legs and paws. The skeletons shake bony hands with big iron ones, and the ogres shake big huge hands with the little sticks of the snow golems. I shake mine with the Witch's, her cold, bony hand in mine. She snatches it back quickly and wipes it on her cloak.

I look back at the room filled with animals and beasties. Max and Mars circle one of the giant spiders, smelling its hairy legs. Mittens, Mr Frost and Blizzard seem fascinated with the bones that make up the skeletons. Saturn and Comet poke little paws at the folds of green skin above the ogres' ankles.

The Witch and I look at each other and nod.

It is time to fight.

CHAPTER 14

The Witch and I hide behind some rocks and look up at the night sky above. The giant chunk of it that has been ripped away eerily lights up the landscape, as if several full moons hang in the sky.

I can't understand what my eyes are seeing. It's as if the Land of Love is a snowglobe and the Megalo has shaken it up and smashed his way in through the top. I hear the sound of drumming, or roaring, and I wonder if that's how Megalos sound.

"It is here, somewhere," the Witch says.

Then, in the distance, we see movement.

The Megalo! I stare in disbelief. It towers over the trees, a giant taller than anything I have ever seen. I am fascinated by its bright white eyes shining down on the forest like spotlights. Its black scaly skin and thick horns. Its huge round body. Its fanged mouth, open, sucking in a pink essence – the power from my land floating up to its mouth.

I look to the Witch, who has gone even paler than usual. A moose charges right past us, and I realize that the drumming sound I hear is thousands of hooves, paws, and wingbeats as the animals of the forests run, slither and fly for their lives, doing all they can to escape!

The Megalo proceeds to suck my world dry. The trees die as their lives are sucked from the roots. The ground turns into a hard, brown cracked surface, as if it hasn't rained for years. The once lush, green forest is now barren – starved, dry land.

The Witch stands, and, with her wand at the ready, she darts

closer to the Megalo. I follow, my mother's wand clenched in my hand.

★★★

"Innoxias!" I shout. I watch as the pink magic flows through the tip of my wand, shimmering in the light of the fire. As my spirit animal takes its tiger form, bright pink with magic, he leaps at the Megalo with his teeth bared and his jaws snapping. He locks onto the Megalo's black, scaly leg.

The Megalo screams in pain, trying to shake off the tiger. The pink tiger is probably ten times the size he was the first time I conjured him, but next to the giant Megalo he still looks like a kitten.

I watch from the behind a boulder as the Megalo pulls my tiger from its leg and throws him to the ground. The bite was enough to distract the Megalo, so it has stopped launching massive fireballs at me and the Witch, at least for a moment. I rise and shout and the tiger rises and charges again.

We've been fighting for hours now. I've used every spell I can think of — even the one to open doors! — but nothing seems to affect the Megalo for long. And every spell drains me of more energy; I'm not sure how much longer I can last.

This Witch, on the other hand, is a wonder. She hasn't slowed down one bit throughout the whole battle, chanting and launching spell after spell at the monster like some kind of one-woman thunderstorm.

But it's becoming clear that even the two of us working together will not be enough to stop this creature. Somehow he has worked up a cyclone, a giant, whirling storm, around himself, so even our biggest blasts miss their mark in all the churning wind.

A sudden **popping** sound from behind me makes me jump, and when I turn I can't believe my eyes. The Wizard! He came back!

"What are you doing here?" I shout, ducking as a fireball flies through the air above.

"I couldn't leave you, Princess. I couldn't just sit back and watch," he replies, releasing a blue fireball of his own from his wand. I duck again as it flies overhead towards the Megalo.

"But what about the Wizard Law?" I send an electrifying pink zap out of my wand into the storm, which has grown even thicker and faster, almost making it impossible to see the Megalo.

"Princess, sometimes rules need to be broken."

And with that, the old Wizard leaps over the boulder and

into swirling winds. I watch as his body is swallowed by the barren dust, his silhouette looking like a shadow puppet as he charges towards the enemy.

The Witch is still chanting, her eyes never leaving the Megalo's. She is engulfed by a black aura; the deepest, darkest magic is possessing her. She calls upon the dark magic of the lost Elder Witches, and each time an Elder comes through, a powerful, jet-black force springs from her body and hits the Megalo, causing it to cry out in pain.

It's working! It's really working!

I battle my way through the storm, ducking as trees and rocks fly past me. I can see the Wizard ahead.

Then I stumble forward and suddenly the winds drop away.

I look around me to find the storm walls spinning around me; we are in the eye of the storm.

The Wizard is using spell after spell on the Megalo, who throws fireballs towards us. The Witch's spirit spider scurries through the storm walls to join the tiger, crawling up the Megalo's body to sink his fangs into the Megalo's scales.

The Megalo grabs the Wizard in its gigantic scaly claw and lifts him off the ground.

"Duratius!" I scream, for the dozenth time, but my magic is just too weak to stun such a big creature. It opens its mouth and begins to suck the power from the Wizard. I watch in horror as the blue magic essence leaves the Wizard's body. The shimmering haze that always surrounded him is gone.

Then the Megalo turns its attention to the Witch's spirit spider, dropping the Wizard on to the ground below with a thud.

I rush over and fall to my knees.

The Wizard is dead.

CHAPTER 15

The Wizard's lifeless, glassy eyes stare up at me as I grab hold of his hands, which are already cold. My eyes fill with tears.

"No! Wake up! Please! You have to wake up!" I grab hold

of the collar of the Wizard's cloak and shake him, his lifeless body like a puppet in my hands.

But he doesn't wake up. He doesn't stir, he doesn't breathe again.

"I'm so sorry," I whisper, through sobbing breaths.

Then I hear the Witch call out, "Amy!"

I look up and see her flying above me, wind-milling her arms and throwing a volley of charged black smoke balls. She barely looks at me and shouts, "Amy, you must keep fighting!"

I turn to find her spirit spider crumpled on the ground, and the Megalo storming towards me.

But I can't move as it approaches. Fear and exhaustion have paralyzed me … and I can't leave the Wizard.

The Megalo stops just a few feet away, looming large above me, a terrible, black mountain of a beast. It opens its mouth, and the white essence starts to cascade down.

This is it. This is how I die.

_"NO!!"_ the Witch screams, and I hear a **popping** sound. Suddenly the Witch is on top of me, pushing me down on the ground. She is using her body as a shield, protecting me.

"Wait! No, stop!" I scream when I realize what she is doing. "Get away!"

But the Witch pushes down on me harder. I look into her eyes and, for just a fraction of a second, I see warmth. I see ... love?

But those eyes fill with pain as the Megalo begins to suck the life from her.

I struggle against the Witch's weight, trying desperately to push her off, to stop her, but it's no use.

Then suddenly she gives up all her strength, and I easily push her off me. Tears sting my eyes as the Witch's lifeless body rolls aside.

She's dead too?

The Megalo, meanwhile, has shifted its attention to my

tiger, who is trying to use his claws to rip into one of the creature's legs.

I reposition the Witch on to her back. I am overcome with emotion. Pain, sorrow, anger. My heart beats fast as I look down at my wicked aunt, the only family I had left.

Before I realize what I am doing, I lay a kiss upon the Witch's forehead and gently close her eyelids.

Something takes over me, a feeling I cannot quite describe. A dangerous mix of wild emotions. I pick up her wand with my free hand, stand up, and advance towards the Megalo.

Anger leads the way.

I feel rage. I feel it swimming in my veins, alongside sorrow – a deadly recipe for revenge. The wands in my hands feel electric, their power vibrating through to my fingers. I feel weightless as I approach the Megalo, breathing through clenched teeth.

The monster turns towards me, and a wild grin grows across its ugly face. It takes a deep breath, but I don't stop walking. It has taken too much from me. I raise both wands, the Witch's in my left, my mother's in my right.

Pointing the wands towards the Megalo's heart, I close my eyes and let the electricity flow from my fingers to my toes, to the top of my head. I feel it surge, taking over my whole body until it has control of me. I feel myself lift, weightless, from the ground.

"Volticlorum trag inoxis, belicari junctio gortilesticar!" I scream. I don't know these words, I don't know where they are coming from. But I keep shouting: *"Ziggarai prituli bajiri!"*

A powerful burst of black and pink erupt from the wands, merging together in front of me to create a deep purple. The blast powers forward and hits the Megalo with such a force it falls backwards, hitting the ground with a mighty thud, causing

the land beneath it to quake. Its body is wrapped in my purple magic; it looks almost like barbed wire, or lightning, coiled around the monster, electrocuting it.

The Megalo screams in pain, writhing on the dusty ground as my magic squeezes life from it. I direct the spell like a musical conductor, zapping the creature without mercy. The Megalo tries to stand, but with a sharp flick from the Witch's wand, the lightning pulls it tighter to the ground. The spell divides, sweeping over the beast like a web, pinning it to the ground and constricting it.

The Megalo struggles as it begins to shrink. I step closer towards it, anger still burning bright in my eyes. It writhes in pain as it withers away, shrinking to the size of an elephant, now a horse, now a dog. Thrashing its claws, it tries to cut through the magical web. Its fireballs instantly dissolve as they touch my spell.

I stand over the Megalo – now the size of a puppy – and the wands vibrate in my hands. It tries to swipe me, it tries to bite me, it tries to suck the power from me, but it's no use. I am stronger. I have the power. And I am not letting it go.

The Megalo, now the size of a guinea pig, continues to shrivel as the storm dies with it. My heart beats fast, the wands feeling hot in my shaking hands, as I guide the spell to keep hold of it.

With a final squeak, the Megalo dissolves before my eyes, leaving just smouldering black powder. The magic still crawls around the powder, and I find that I can't drop my arms. I can't end the spell. Tears spring to my eyes and slowly – very slowly – the anger begins to fade.

My arms begin to shake as the magic lessens, becomes thinner. Finally, I drop the wands, ending the spell, and bury my head in my hands.

★★★

The world is quiet, the storm gone. The only sounds are my sniffling nose and choking sobs. I look at the forest, destroyed by the Megalo.

When I defeated the Darkness Hex, the magic erased the mess, restoring the Land of Love to its normal radiance. But now the world has not gone back to normal. It remains tainted. Scarred.

I look at the wands, my mother's and the Witch's, and I look at the palm of my hands. Each has four tiny crescent-shaped marks where I dug my nails in, grasping the wands so tightly.

"You did it, child." I feel a cold hand upon my shoulder. I turn, and—

"Aaarrrrghh!!!!" I scream. It's the Witch! "A g-g-ghost!"

The Witch rolls her eyes. "I'm not a ghost, you silly girl."

"But ... you're dead!" I shout, my eyes growing wide.

"I thought so too," she replies, taking her hat off and beating the dust from it. "Turns out I'm a lot tougher than I knew."

I suddenly have a thought. "Wait! Does that mean…?"

I leap up and run towards the body of the Wizard, almost tripping on my own feet.

"Wizard! Wake up! Wake up, it's over!" I gently shake him.

The Wizard's lifeless body remains still.

"Wizard!" I cry. "You have to wake up now!"

"He's gone," the Witch says.

"No! You're still alive! Why can't he be too?" Tears now streaking down my face, I bury my face in the Wizard's soft silky robes.

I pick up his broken glasses and place them gently over his eyes. "He can't see without his glasses," I cry.

As I adjust them over his nose, the Wizard's body begins to

glow. Confused, I stand and watch as he begins to rise, light

shining from within, to the clouds

above.

"What's happening?" I

whisper.

"He is leaving us now,"

the Witch replies.

The Wizard rises up and

up, slowly fading away until

there is nothing to see but the early

morning sun.

★★★

The Witch and I walk back to the house in silence. Although

the battle has been won, I feel I have lost. As I spot my home

peeking over the horizon, a thought occurs to me:

"You saved my life," I say, stopping in my tracks.

The Witch also stops and turns back towards me, avoiding my eyes. She says nothing.

"You sacrificed yourself to save me."

Her cheeks blush – a touch of pale pink against her ghostly white skin.

I suddenly find myself throwing myself on to her, clinging to her as I embrace the Witch in a hug I never thought possible. Her arms outstretched, I feel her body flinch at my touch. But, after a few seconds, I feel her stiff arms awkwardly pat my head and hold me too.

"There, there child," she soothes softly.

We stand there together in the eerie, post-battle morning as the birds return to the world, chirping happily.

The Witch suddenly pulls away with a force that makes me stumble backwards.

"Urgh, enough of that gross stuff," she spits, wiping my germs from her cloak. "I'm going to fetch my beasties and get out of here. Make your own way back."

And with a **pop**, she is gone.

And I notice that my tiara is gone too.

CHAPTER 16

"Good morning, Amy," says Grandfather Oak.

"Good morning, Grandfather," I reply.

I sit in front of my tree, hugging my knees. When I got home earlier, the beasties had already been retrieved by the Witch, and I was greeted by an avalanche of lovely animals and golems, all licking and nuzzling and pawing and hugging me. Now I'm just exhausted, but I can't go rest without first checking on my friend.

I tell Grandfather Oak everything. About the Megalo, about the Wizard's death, about how I managed to defeat him. "But

I don't understand something," I say. "When I picked up the Witch's wand, and I had my mother's too, a weird feeling came over me. And I used a spell I was never taught; I don't know where it came from. But it worked, whatever it was."

Grandfather Oak smiles. "My dear, from what I can gather, you experienced the most powerful emotions that exist. The Wizard's heroic death brought you tremendous sorrow. And the Witch's death – as far as you believed it – brought you anger, confusion, grief ... and love."

I wrinkle my nose. "Love? She hates me!"

Grandfather Oak chuckles. "Yes, she does. But deep down, Amy, she also has love for you. She sacrificed her own life to save you. Only a true love can do that. And with all those emotions brewing inside you, and the wand of black magic with your mother's wand of white magic, you were able to use the two forces of good and evil to your advantage and defeat the Megalo."

I ponder this for a moment or two. My heart aches for the old Wizard. And I feel a huge responsibility now to make sure his sacrifice will be worth it.

And I think of the Witch's sacrifice. "The Witch and I hugged," I mumble.

"Yes? How did that feel?"

"Weird," I answer. "She wants me dead, Grandfather – she said it herself. And now that this is over, she'll try to take over the land again. The only way that will happen is if I am dead."

"She is a tricky one, that's for sure. She has been very hurt in the past, and that pain turned to anger. She became a wicked creature because of it. Sometimes I like to imagine a little light bulb in all of us. When it's bright, we are happy. And sometimes that little light flickers, when we feel sad or angry. The light gets dimmer when we are depressed, and at times the light goes completely out, leaving us in darkness. I believe the Witch has lived in darkness for a very long time. But seeing you in

159

danger … her light flickered. Maybe just a little flicker, but it reminded her of emotions she had long forgotten. Perhaps now, her light is shining ever so slightly."

"My light doesn't feel very bright right now," I say.

"And that is OK too. We are all meant to feel emotions, and you, my dear, have felt many of them in the past few days. Everyone's light goes off from time to time. But why do you think you were able to destroy the Megalo?"

"Because I had good and bad magic?"

"Well, you used your emotions. The most powerful magic comes from emotions. You felt an anger deep inside you, and dark magic was brewing through it. Mixed with the goodness of your heart, you created a new magic. Combined the two forces."

"So being angry is good?"

"Being angry is very good. And being sad is very good. Without them, we would never really know happiness." Grandfather Oak smiles.

"What's going to happen with the Witch now?" I wonder.

"I don't know, Amy. But I think you have turned her little light on. How she deals with that now … who knows. But you have shown her that she can love again."

I ponder this for a moment or two. Perhaps Grandfather Oak is right. Maybe the Witch will change and we can become … friends? Who knows. All I know is that nothing will ever be the same again.

"Never abandon yourself, Amy. You may feel lost and confused as your past is slowly coming into focus, but don't let that change who you are." My old tree smiles, and I do my best to smile back.

I pick myself up and wipe the dirt from my knees. Noticing the luscious red roses that decorate the front of my house, I decide to dedicate them to my mum and dad.

EPILOGUE

It won't be long now, my children, it won't be long now. That silly, pink-haired twerp had it all along. I should have known her father would have left it to her somehow!

But now I have it. The Sun Diamond from her tiara. And I know exactly what to do with it.

First things first: the Book of Prophecies. Yes, my lovely book, a final, precious inheritance from the Elder Witches. The prophecies are all well and good, but the true treasure is in the packaging. Here, right on the cover, they embedded the Sea Sapphire.

Two beautiful, glowing gems. Two out of three.

It's been a long time since all three precious jewels have been together. The longest time, in fact. Not since the very beginning, the founding of magic in this world. The Founder Prince's crown, forged with magic most pure.

Magic most powerful.

Magic that will soon be mine.

So all I need is the third precious stone. The Fire Ruby.

Ready or not, dear ruby, here I come.

But where is it?

Check out this other book featuring Amy Lee and her friends and family!